Canción Mixteca — My Father's Version

¡Qué lejos estoy del pueblo donde he nacido!
Inmensa nostalgia invade mi pensamiento
Y al verme tan solo y triste cual hoja al viento
Quisiera llorar, quisiera morir de sentimiento

¡O Tierra del Sol, me muero por verte!
Yo aquí tan lejos viviendo sin luz ni calor
Y al verme tan solo y triste cual hoja al viento
Quisiera llorar, quisiera morir de sentimiento

José López Alavés, 1915

A Juana — AR

Text copyright © 2019 by Elisa Amado
Illustrations copyright © 2019 by Alfonso Ruano
Published in Canada and the USA in 2019 by Groundwood Books

Groundwood Books / House of Anansi Press
groundwoodbooks.com

We gratefully acknowledge for their financial support of our publishing program the
Canada Council for the Arts, the Ontario Arts Council and the Government of Canada.

Canada Council **Conseil des Arts**
for the Arts **du Canada**

ONTARIO ARTS COUNCIL
CONSEIL DES ARTS DE L'ONTARIO
an Ontario government agency
un organisme du gouvernement de l'Ontario

With the participation of the Government of Canada | **Canada**
Avec la participation du gouvernement du Canada

Library and Archives Canada Cataloguing in Publication
Title: My friend / Elisa Amado ; pictures by Alfonso Ruano.
Names: Amado, Elisa, author. | Ruano, Alfonso, illustrator.
Identifiers: Canadiana (print) 2018906692X | Canadiana (ebook) 20189066938 |
ISBN 9781554989393 (hardcover) | ISBN 9781554989409 (EPUB) |
ISBN 9781773062754 (Kindle)
Classification: LCC PS8551.M335 M94 2019 | DDC jC813/.6—dc23

The illustrations were made with watercolors on paper.
Design by Michael Solomon
Printed and bound in Malaysia

My Friend

Elisa Amado

Pictures by Alfonso Ruano

 GROUNDWOOD BOOKS
HOUSE OF ANANSI PRESS
TORONTO   BERKELEY

I knew you would be my best friend the day I came to school the first time.

Right away you understood so much about me. And I understood you.

I didn't know too much about shows on TV but soon I could guess which ones you liked the best and I watched them, too.

And when I bought you a present at the corner store, I was sure you'd love it. And you did.

You gave me your favorite book to read, and I read it all the way through, even though it was hard. After I finally finished it I told you, cross my heart and hope to die, that now it's my favorite book, too.

I am so lucky I found you. I know you and you know me. That is why we are best friends forever.

When kids at school laugh and say to
you, "How can you hang out with her?
She is so weird," you just say, "Who cares?
We're best friends. Is that a problem?"

And if new kids who are more like me say,
"Why are you hanging out with her? She doesn't
understand us. She's one of them," I always say,
"You are wrong. You don't know her. I do. And
she knows me. She is my best friend."

One day, you came to dinner at my house. My parents knew you were my best friend, so they made my favorite dinner and set the table as though it was a holiday. And you got all dressed up.

I could tell you didn't like the food so much. You had trouble finishing your dinner. But that was okay. You'd never eaten our kind of food before.

And you didn't know the kinds of things we always do at dinner. You didn't know that my father always shouts and gets mad about things that he has read that day. And that we sometimes shout back at him in our language. You didn't know that my mother gets mad at us for shouting and arguing and complains if we don't eat our food.

But I could see that you were really trying to understand what was going on and to be extra polite, even when there was so much noise and arguing. At first I was kind of embarrassed but then I thought to myself, you are my best friend, it's okay.

But then my dad put on his favorite CD. And he began to sing along as loud as he could. It's the song that makes us remember where we were before we came here and what it was like. Sometimes I feel like crying when I hear that song.

When we went back to my bedroom you began to laugh. "That was so weird!" you said.

I felt like dying.

And soon you got up and said, "I'd better go home." And asked my mother to call your mother to come and pick you up. It was still early.

That night I cried. My parents kept asking me, "What's wrong?"

"I want to go home. I hate it here!" I shouted.

"We can't go back. We have no choice," my father said. "Just be glad you are safe and stop whining. It could be a lot worse."

You were my best friend. I know you and I thought you knew me. I listen to your music all the time. Even if I don't like it. But you laughed at mine.

At school I eat the same food you do. Every day. Even if it's strange. But you don't even notice how strange it is for me. And even though you tried I could tell that you didn't really like our food.

You don't know anything about me!

I played my song over and over. I was so mad at you that I never wanted to see you again. Finally I fell asleep.

When I woke up, I had to go to school. I didn't want to go. You were my best friend and now I was all alone. I knew you and I thought you knew me. But it isn't true. You don't really know me at all.

But my parents made me go anyway.

As I walked down the street, I felt really bad. If you don't know me, I thought, no one in this whole place knows me. What will happen to me when I have no best friend?

Then I saw you standing in front of the school.
 I started to remember.
That on the first day of school you came right up to me and asked my name.
That you sat next to me every day.
That you told people who made fun of my clothes, "Drop dead! She's way cooler than you."
That you called me every night and talked to me about everything that happened that day.
Then you turned around and smiled. "Hey. Thanks for dinner. I really had fun."

"Hey," I said. And we walked in
the door together.
Best friends.

Mixteca Song — My Translation

We're so far away from our home where we were born.
It makes us feel sad all over.
And when we see ourselves blowing in the wind like autumn leaves,
we feel so sad and alone we feel like crying, almost like dying.

O sunny place, we want to see you again so badly.
We are here all alone without your light and warmth.
And when we see ourselves blowing in the wind like autumn leaves,
we feel so sad and alone we feel like crying, almost like dying.

This is what I think our favorite family song sounds like in English.

An Indigenous man from Oaxaca, José López Alavés, wrote this song when he was far from home in northern Mexico. At my house we sing our own version in Spanish. It might sound silly in English but for us, in Spanish, it's exactly how we feel about living so far from the home that we left behind, that we miss.